FROGGY GOES TO GRANDMA'S

FROGGY GOES TO GRANDMA'S

by JONATHAN LONDON

illustrated by FRANK REMKIEWICZ

VIKING

For "Grandma Cook" & "Grandma Sitting Rich"
& "Nana" and for Regina, Chef Aaron, Sean, Eli,
and sweet Maureen
—J.L.

For Nana Silvia, Farmor Bente,
Granny Annie, and Nanabird
—F.R.

VIKING
Penguin Young Readers Group
An imprint of Penguin Random House LLC
375 Hudson Street
New York, New York 10014

First published in the United States of America by Viking, an imprint of Penguin Random House LLC, 2017

Text copyright © 2017 by Jonathan London
Illustrations copyright © 2017 by Frank Remkiewicz

LIBRARY OF CONGRESS CATALOGING-IN-PUBLICATION DATA IS AVAILABLE
ISBN: 9781101999646

Manufactured in China   Set in ITC Kabel Std   These illustrations were made with watercolor

10   9   8   7   6   5   4   3   2   1

Froggy woke up
and bounced on his bed—*boing! boing! boing!*
"Yippee!" he sang.
"We're going to Grandma's!"
And he jumped off . . .

WEEEEEEEE!

and got dressed—*zip! zoop! zup! zut! zut! zut! zat!*

FRROOGGYY!

called his mother.
"Wha-a-a-a-t?"
"It's time to pack for our trip, dear!"
"I already *di-i-i-i-d*!" he said.

Then he flopped into the kitchen—
flop flop flop—
and ate his breakfast of cereal and flies—
munch crunch munch.

Then off to the taxi they went—
flop flop flop.

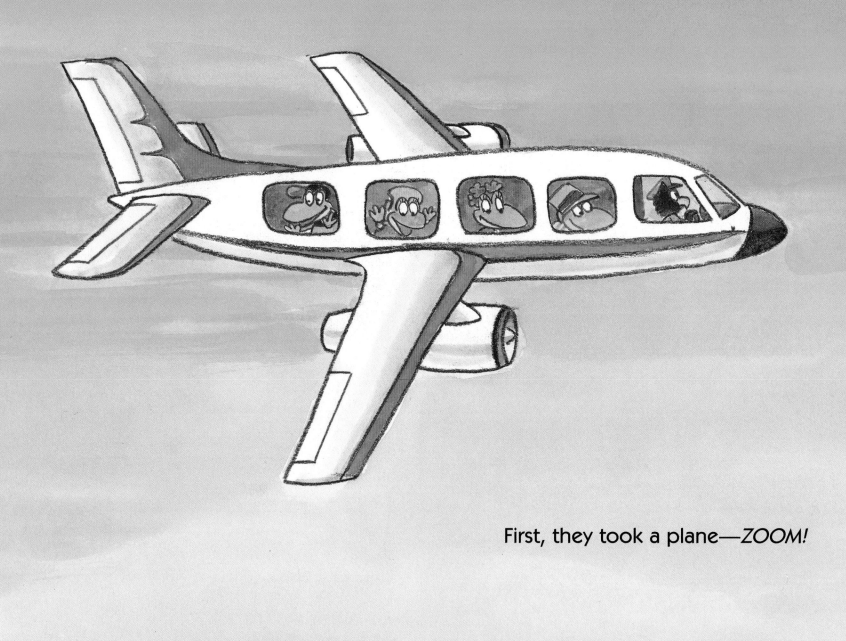

First, they took a plane—*ZOOM!*

Then they went by taxi again—*BEEP! BEEP!*
"I can't wait to see Grandma Cook!" cried Froggy.
(He called her "Grandma Cook" because
she was the best cook in the world!)

When they finally got to Grandma's,
he cried, "Grandma! Grandma! Grandma Cook!"
And he leapfrogged over Dad.
He leapfrogged over Mom.
He leapfrogged over Pollywogilina . . .

and almost knocked
Grandma down.

"Whoa!" cried Grandma Cook.
"You're too big to catch, Muffin!
But you're just the right size
for a great big hug!"

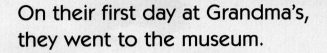

On their first day at Grandma's,
they went to the museum.

"Now remember, Muffin,
no yelling and bouncing
around!" said Grandma.

"Look!" yelled Froggy, bouncing over to a painting. "The famous Frogga Lisa by Leonardo da Piggy!"

FRROOGGYY!

called Grandma.
"Wha-a-a-a-t?"
"Don't touch it!"
But he was already racing to a
statue of an alligator named
The Thinker.
"Look!" yelled Froggy . . .

and he sat with his chin on his fist
and said, "I'm thinking. I think."
"I think you stink!" said Polly, giggling.
"We don't say 'stink,'" said Grandma.
"We say 'smell.'"
"Pee-*yoo!*" said Polly, holding her nose.

The next day, they went to a baseball game.
"Yippee!" cried Froggy.
Just then, the batter hit a pop-up—*whack!*—
and the ball sailed up . . . up . . . up . . .
"It's *mine*!" cried Froggy.

And he leapfrogged over Grandma.
He leapfrogged over the dugout.
He leapfrogged over the catcher . . .
and caught it in his baseball cap.
"Got it!" cried Froggy.

Then he put his cap back on
(with the ball still in it)—*BOINK!*—

and knocked himself down.
"OUT!" cried the ump.
"Oops!" said Froggy.

The next night, they went to
the amusement park.
Grandma didn't like high places,
but Froggy said, "Come on, Grandma,
it's as easy as falling off a log!"

And they went on a water slide
called The Logger's Revenge.
But when they got to the top . . .

Grandma threw up her hands
and yelled *"WHEEEEEEEEEEE!"*—
and Froggy yelled "Yikes!" looking
greener than normal.

And on the day after that,
Grandma took them bowling
(her favorite sport).
First up, Grandma bowled the ball . . .

"STRIKE!"

Next up, Polly *pushed* the ball,
and it rolled slowly . . . slowly . . .

and came to a stop against the front pin.
"STWIKE!" yelled Polly.

Now it was Froggy's turn.
"Watch this!" cried Froggy.
And he threw the ball with all his might,
but his fingers got stuck . . .

and he *flew* with the ball! *"YIIIIIIIIIKES!"*
THUMP!
"Oops!" cried Froggy.
"Good try," said Grandma.

But the best day of all—was the last day.
Grandma Cook was going to *cook!*
"I want to help!" cried Froggy.
Then Froggy stood on a chair
and helped her stir the sauce,
and he sang—
"Swirly girly swiggly SPLASH!"
"Now it's time to boil the
spaghetti," said Grandma.

"*I'll* open it!" said Froggy.
And he was so excited, he tore open the box—
RIIIIIIIIIIIP!
Spaghetti flew everywhere—
and rained down on Polly's head.

WAAAAAAAA!

wailed Polly.

"Oops!" cried Froggy, looking more red in the face than green.

But soon Grandma Cook served her famous "pasta froginaise"—otherwise known as spaghetti with fly sauce!

And Froggy and Polly chowed down.

"YUM!" cried Froggy.
"You're the best grandma *ever!*"
Sluuuuurp sluuuuurp sluuuuuuurp!